William Yergin

Tact and talent and other poems

William Yergin

Tact and talent and other poems

ISBN/EAN: 9783337137458

Printed in Europe, USA, Canada, Australia, Japan

Cover: Foto ©Andreas Hilbeck / pixelio.de

More available books at **www.hansebooks.com**

TACT AND TALENT,

AND

OTHER POEMS.

BY

W. C. YERGIN.

Lehrer der deutschen Sprache.

CONTENTS.

Press of the Pioneer,
Big Rapids, Mich.

Tact and Talent.

What is Tact and what is Talent?
  Ask yourself these questions, friend;
For you need both Tact and Talent
  For life's mighty dividend.

Talent's something worth the having.
  True.   But Tact is ev'rything.
Talent gives you power, attention;
  Tact will roses round you fling.

Talent's sober, grave and weighty;
  Tact is all of this and more:
It's the life of all your senses,
  And its gold within the ore.

Tact is useful in all places
  And it's useful at all times,—
You may ring your bell of Talent,
  But your Tact makes sweeter chimes.

Tact in solitude is useful,
  For it shows a man the world:
And it bears aloft his ensign,
  If that ensign is unfurled.

Talent gives a man his power,
　　Tact to him gives ready skill;
Talent gives the weight and sternness,
　　Tact, celerity and skill.

Talent knows what needs the doing
　　Tact knows how—aye, that and more;
Plans, constructs, adorns the building;
　　Graces service at the door.

Wealth is Talent in a bundle,
　　Ready Tact is ten to one;
Talent is the wealth that's hoarded,
　　Tact the circulating sum.

Take them in the social circle
　　Where is seen a wealth of grace;
Talent takes a part dramatic,
　　Tact distorts most ev'ry face.

And 'twill keep you in good humor,
　　Ev'ry night the whole week through;
But dramatic Talent whispers,
　　"Murder! ha! they're after you!"

Tragedies can give no pleasure,
　　When the actors lack of Tact;
But combine the two together
　　And they give a taking act.

There's dramatic Tact and Talent,
　　And of them is little lack;
But they seldom are together
　　At a time upon one track.

So we have successful pieces
 Which are not respectable;
And, reversely, to be truthful,
 Which is more electable.

Taken at the bar of justice
 Where they work in rivalry,
Talent sees the journey ended,
 Tact's the first one in from sea.

Talent oft is complimented
 When 'tis pleading at the bar;
But for Tact the vict'ry's certain:
 All is won while yet afar.

Talent makes the world to wonder,
 Tact is more astonishment;
For it has no weight to carry
 And is never falsely bent.

It has sail when wind is moving
 Matters not from where it blows;
It keeps eye upon the dial
 And it knows just how it goes.

Take them into church a Sunday,
 Talent speaks in words of worth;
But to Tact twice ears are eager
 For the words before their birth.

Talent can obtain a living,
 Tact will make one anywhere;
Talent wins a goodly title,
 Tact receives one far more fair.

Talent honors to profession,
  Tact gains honor to the same;
Talent feels the weight it carries,
  Tact moves nimbly—ne'er is lame.

Take them in the senate chamber,
  Talent has the ears of all;
Tact wins hearts and captures voters,
  And it knows just when to call.

Talent's voice may be commanding,
  Tact is one that is obeyed;
Talent's honored with approval,
  But for Tact the choice is made.

Tact seems filled with ev'ry wisdom
  Yet it looks not wondrous wise;
Ever seems all plain and common
  But awakens your surprise.

Energy.

"What is energy or power?"
  Once was asked an aged man
By a youth who sought for knowledge,—
  Worthy purpose, noble plan.

And the old man, full of wisdom,
  Slowly laid aside his book
And from o'er his long-worn glasses
  Gave the youth an earnest look.

When his quizzing look was answered,
　　He began in accents clear
To explain about the matter
　　Which the youth desired to hear.

" Now my young man," said the elder,
　　" Lend your ears and give good heed;
And I'll give to you this knowledge,
　　Hoping that you may succeed.

" Energy is application,
　　Perseverance, industry
In whatever you're pursuing;
　　And it means activity.

" Nothing great can be accomplished
　　Without constant, active toil:
Motion is a law of nature,
　　Seedling in a fertile soil.

" Lack of action portrays dying,
　　If it is not death itself;
And when man becomes inactive
　　He is laid upon the shelf.

" See, to-day, the hugest engines
　　Gracing to Invention's hour!
These would be in fault, and useless,
　　If they had no moving power.

" But awaken steam within them
　　And they puff and snort and roar;
Take you over land and water,
　　Land you on a foreign shore.

" Energy is steam and power,
    And the motive part of mind;
And is never lacking in the
    Truly cultured and refined.

" 'Tis, my friend, the force propelling.
    This to you I'll demonstrate
By a common law of physics,
    If it isn't yet too late.

"All transformed can be momentum,
    To velocity, you know,
As to quantity of matter.
    Prove it, and you'll find it so.

"Now, for instance, take a body,
    Small, and driven by great force;
Then reverse the situation
    And pursue the selfsame course.

"Now the same force will move slower
    Increased quantity, you'll find.
And you'll see the smaller body
    Will the larger leave behind.

"So it is in Metaphysics,—
    The extent of human power
May be changed into degrees of
    High endowment, hour by hour.

" Yes, I see," the young man answered;
    And he turned to go away.
"But, my friend, what is your hurry?
    Linger yet five minutes, pray."

" Very well; though time is precious
    To me as to ev'ry man."
" Yet how few that realize this
    In their race to lead the van.

" But—returning to our topic—
    So it is with lesser brain;
It quite often leave great talent,
    Constant action makes it gain.

"Firm, undaunted, ceaseless vigor,
    Is the principle in man
Which give strength and vim to effort
    When he steps and says, ' I can!'

"And 'tis this which gives him genius
    And that quality of mind
Bursting forth in manly vigor;
    Oftimes rather hard to find.

"This is what meets opposition,
    And defies and bears it down;
Gives to man his greatest prestige;
    Wins for him his golden crown.

"This, you note, is quite peculiar
    Of those famous intellects
That secure a name in hist'ry,
    And to whom we pay respects.

"And they are the men of action,
    Pioneers of thought and deed,
Who originate, discover,
    What is often greatest need.

"And they overturn old orders,
　　Always building up anew;
And, reverse old wornout systems.
　　Such is that which you should do.

"To this class belong Columbus,
　　Fulton, Watt and Washington;
Henry Clay, and B. J. Franklin,—
　　Noble men who've nobly done."

"Yes," replied the young man gravely,
　　"These live but in history;
But to-day, to be successful,
　　One must work quite diff'rently."

"True, perhaps, but wait a moment
　　And I'll tell you something plain;
Though the present time is harder,
　　One must still have lots of brain.

"And I think, to tell you truly,
　　If the youth of our to-day
Had the principles of greatness,
　　That the world would give them way.

"You have other thoughts of greatness
　　Than some youth of whom I know:
To be great in deed and action
　　Is true wisdom from the go.

"One can't load one's self with habits
　　And preserve the energy;
That, makes one too much impeded
　　Ever truly great to be."

13

"Well, good sir, your words are wisdom;
And I thank you ere I go.
I will strive to profit by them;
For they're good advice I know.

❧ ❧ ❧

Thinking Makes the Man.

Thinking marks the highest manhood
In this busy world of ours;
So develop thought and judgment,
In advance of muscle powers.

Many men to-day are children
From the fact they cannot think.
On through life they plod and hobble,
Each one but a rusty link.

Constitution may be settled,
But the judgment immature;
Muscles round and strong and hardened,
But the reason insecure.

Many ones can run and wrestle,
Work hard in the field all day;
But they can't observe or reason,
For they do not think that way.

Custom self to thinking deeply,
And when reading understand;
Else you may be far in ocean
When you'd rather be on land.

If a book is read with hurry,
  'Tis a most confusing task;
But to read the while digesting,
  Takes away each mystic mask.

If your reading wakes no thinking,
  Either lacks the book or you.
If the book, take up another;
  If yourself, exchange that too.

Some have stores of book-gained knowl
    edge ·
  And are not e'en worldly wise;
But a knowledge wise and active
  Is the knowledge that we prize.

You may read, perhaps remember,
  Without knowing what you read;
But your health will be the better
  If it's food on which you feed.

For your health, 'tis more conducive
  Not to eat another meal
Till the one has been digested
  And again you hungry feel.

And 'tis just as beneficial
  Not to read another book,
Or leave one page for another
  Till it's yours in ev'ry nook.

"Join your thinking with your reading,"
   Is a maxim learned with ease;
And to do so is an action
   That is always sure to please.

But a man is not a thinker
   Who can reason only then;
Nor is he, whose mind is vacant
   As he walks life's traversed glen.

Therefore, rest not that your thinking
   Is as circumstances bid;
But before they come be active,
   Then you've done as Lincoln did.

Guard your thoughts and train them
   rightly,
   Lest they wild and useless run;
Then when life draws to its closing,
   You will hear the words, " Well done."

Do you know the art of thinking?
   If you don't, just try and learn;
And begin by reading maxims,
   For they always do their turn.

And they are the pith of logic,
   Methodizing memory—
Standing to support your statement,
   If that statement truthful be.

Mind by cause is ever active,
  Even when you're fast asleep;
But it wanders desultory
  If no guard o'er it you keep.

Watch your thoughts, and this will teach
    you
  What, and when, and how to think;
And your work will be the better
  If you can this knowledge drink.

Mind can work to better purpose
  When it knows just what to do.
Its your servant or your master;
  You rule it, or it rules you.

All it knows from other sources,
  You can cause to be a gain:
For its work is not all grinding,
  It can sow the golden grain.

It is only by grave thinking
  That a man can know himself;
Yet without this, other knowledge
  Isn't worth to him an elf.

So look in your mind more closely
  Till you know your own true worth.
Thus conceit and ignorance, shall
  Bring to you no blasting dearth.

Yet not reading makes you wiser;
　It's the power you have to think
Raises you into the highlands
　Far above the swamp's low brink.

Thinking then is what makes manhood;
　As you think you always are.
You can't rise above your thinking
　At your home, or when afar.

Thinking rightly is self culture;
　'Tis the germ of action true:
And the thought's before the action
　Whether good or what you do.

Purity of thought makes purpose:
　Place your standard very high:
Stake your claim where gold is plenty;
　For you get just what you buy.

Mind the Glory of Man.

Mind to man is crowning glory
　When calm reason holds its sway,
But dethrone fair, regal reason,—
　Lo! the glory fades away.

No possession so productive
　If but cultivated right;
Other charm is never greater
　In Time's ever onward flight,

Wealth and birth and rank you may have,
　Live in luxury and ease,
Be a teacher or a cobbler,
　Work for self or whom you please.

But your being cross and crabbed
　Shows at once you've lost your mind;
For when reason is the ruler,
　You are wise, and good, and kind.

Wealth and birth, official station
　May be, rank far up with you;
But these cannot have the rev'rence
　That to mind is always due.

Cultivated mind and morals,
　Not apart, but blent in one,
Ever have respectful tribute
　And in life, are like the sun.

But so few of young men starting
　At the ladder's bottom round,
Ever get beyond its middle;
　And for this some fault is found.

But they had not calculated
　And could not have started right
Or they would have climbed the ladder,
　Keeping mind within their sight.

Thinking and not show makes manhood,
　Though the most are all for show;
And parade about their learning,
　But alone can learning go?

Take an engine and a boiler,
  Generate in one your steam
And the two will work together:
  But will one horse make a team?

Great success means toilsome culture
  All along some given line;
But if you shall hide your talent,
  It will go to swell the nine.

This is but the law of Nature
  And her laws are always just.
She bestows all kinds of treasure,
  But they're found beneath the dust.

Greatest men are men of action,
  Thinking into action goes;
But wrong action and wrong thinking
  Brings to us our greatest woes.

Nature plants within each bosom
  Principles of excellence;
But they must be cultivated,
  Or they're not worth half a pence.

As the grand and splendid rivers
  Rolling onward to the sea,
Owe their strength to spring and brook-
    let
  From the mountain and the lea,

So, does wide and sweeping power
To distinguished people, come
From the springlets of self culture
That of all life are the sum.

You perhaps are poor, a stranger,
That is nothing in your way;
Captain Cook, a famous sailor,
Started from a hut of clay.

Fifty years was famed Lord Eldon
In the British parliament;
He was but a merchant's scion
But upon self culture bent.

Franklin, diplomat and statesman,
Was in youth a printer's lad;
And a penny roll or biscuit
At the noon was all he had.

Goldsmith, Johnson, many others,
Once were pressed—in need of gold:
But that did not stop their action,
Can you stop the heat or cold?

Gird then, friend, for self instruction,
Set high price upon your time;
Then your tho'ts that will be purchased
Will be thoughts that are sublime.

Thoughts of greatness come by reading
　　Books that teach the way of life;
And we rise by overcoming,
　　Being active in the strife.

If you wish for wealth and greatness,
　　Do the little kindly deed;
And give something to your neighbor
　　If your neighbor is in need.

✤ ✤ ✤

Pride and Humility.

How often human nature looks
　　Up to the wealthy man of pride
Because it envies him his gold,
　　His social circle gay and wide.

But notice now the lilies fair;
　　They neither toil, nor sow, nor spin
And yet they teach a higher life
　　To him who has a soul within.

The flowers, fair and innocent,
　　Yield to the air a fragrant breath;
They're clustered oft upon the bier
　　And light approaching shades of death

Yet many say, How happy he
  Who has of plenty to be proud;
Who moves 'neath golden canopy,
  With Fame a pleasant shading cloud.

And happy he whose genius wins
  Each bargain which he undertakes;
But such is not true brotherhood
  When thirst by brother's blood he slakes.

And such is not true happiness;
  For long as life's years onward roll,
Dark phantoms haunt, unto the grave,
  The one who dares to crush a soul.

True happiness is like the buds,
  And it will blossom in our lives
If we but plant within our hearts
  That kindly loves which never dies.

There is a story of two men
  Who sought the temple, once to pray;
One was a rigid Pharisee,
  But which was justified that day?

Or which is truer, nobler mind?
  And which makes one the better man?
A thinking as the Pharisee
  Or like the humble publican?

At all events, the humble man
  Remembers he is lowly clay
And thinks of how much worse he is
  Than those he meets with ev'ry day.

He reads and loves to think about
  Those men who tower far above
In wisdom, goodness, courage, grace,
  And all the noble ways of love.

And thus his mind is filled with thoughts
  That ever teach him how to live
And always how to be alike
  The flow'rs that pleasant honey give.

The proud man thinks, How rich I am;
  And wiser, better than my friends;
He watches close the wid'ning gulf,
  But cares no whit about the ends.

He, ever deep in love with self,
  Feeds his conceit at others loss
And fills his mind with subtle thoughts
  Which cover poison with sweet gloss.

Now both these men have their reward.
  The humble man as years roll on
Becomes more noble, wise and good,—
  His life advances like the dawn.

The other man gains greater wealth
  Of gold, but ever dwarfs his mind
Until a shriveled frosted thing
  Is all ambition leaves behind.

Might and Right.

One eve, a man of quiet mien
Within a village hall was seen.
'Twas in the autumn of the year
When leaves were red, and gold, and sere.

He did not come, as some men do,
With pomp and state and much ado;
But like the morning light he came, -
And thus he ever seemed the same.

The people from the country near
Were in the hall that they might hear.
The bills had said, " Exactly eight;"
And not a person entered late.

Then, stepping to the platform's hight,
" My words," quoth he, " are for the right.
I'm not arrayed 'gainst any man,
Nor do I stand for clique or clan.

" But men are fooling breath away
O'er current issues of the day.
Two wrongs, they say, don't make a right;
And yet all parties arm for fight.

" They haul, and pull, and saw about;
For this and that man raise a shout;
And say that times are getting worse
And money's less within our purse.

"Now let me tell you something, friends:
These, do not lead to highest ends.
But if the people all were good,
You each would help each all you could.

"And if all men were without guile,
They'd never wear deceiving smile;
Nor ever hate, or cheat, or steal,
And plan against their neighbors' weal.

"They'd never gamble, drink or chew,
Nor do the things our Lord won't do;
They'd not kneel down in church and pray,
Then quarrel the balance of the day.

"Nor can these errors be repressed,
Nor any evil be redressed
By making laws to force a man
To follow after better plan.

"Though men, who in the pulpit stand,
Are voicing loud o'er all the land,
That, if on Sunday one saws wood,
Just legislate and make him good!

"This principle is all at fault.
The law may cause a man to halt;
But in his mind he thinks the same
And may be plans to dodge its claim.

"Pure, earnest love to God and man
Has been the law since time began.
And when by love men think and do,
They will be good and times good too.

"The people came to Christ one day
 With stones, to crush a life away;
 And said, Good sir, this woman, here,
 Hath sinned. Wilt thou make sentence
  clear?

" He, stooping down, wrote in the sand.
 The stones fell out of each one's hand;
 And feeling guilt, they slunk away
 Because they, too, had sinned that day.

" But Christ nowhere will sin uphold,
 Outside the gate or in the fold.
 And, though these men accused her, sore,
 He sweetly said, Go, sin no more!

" But he has died that you might live
 And longs to pardon and forgive;
 And, impart strength that you may choose
 The good, and ev'ry wrong refuse.

"Oh come, while it is yet to-day!
 Oh come, cries he, Turn not away!
 Trust me, when crushing wrong is rife
 And you shall have eternal life."

The Mount of Miseries.

While looking through a book one day,
  A reader old and worn,
I chanced upon a page all marked,
  Its corners crimped and torn.

I always like to look at scrip,
  And study every trace;
For these portray the character
  As does the human face.

Upon this page began some prose
  With title as this lay;
'Twas written many years ago;
  It opened in this way:—

While seated in my elbow-chair
  To think grave thoughts and deep,
The curtains of my vision rolled
  And I was fast asleep.

And as I slept my fancy woke,
  And pleasant was my dream;
For I was wafted far away
  Beyond times flowing stream.

And there I saw all kinds of flow'rs,
  The countless angel band;
But no departed souls up there
  From out our lower land.

I looked around all wonderment,
    And saw a native near—
" Will you explain this mystery,
    That doth to some appear?"

" How readest thou?" the answer came;
    " Doth not the Bible say
That David's not in heaven yet,
    But waits the final day?

" In death, all sleep beneath the dust,
    This fact none can decry;
For ' each and ev'ry soul that sins,'
    God says, ' shall surely die.' "

And then the scene began to change,
    New things came into view;
And when upon the earth once more,
    Old thoughts were changed for new.

Methought I saw upon this sphere,
    A broad expansive plain
Where naught but grass and mosses grew,
    Instead of golden grain.

And as I looked I heard a voice
    To mankind speak and say,
" Come, throw your burdens on this plain
    Nor wait another day!"

Quite near the center was a place
    On which I took my stand,
That I might see the people come
    From out each border land.

And, as I stood, from ev'rywhere
  Came people young and old--
Each threw away a diff'rent load,
  One threw away his gold.

Ere long, this pile grew mountain high
  And many miles around;
For in it were thrown all defects
  That 'mongst mankind are found.

There was a certain woman there,
  Of thin and airy shape;
Who acted very solemnly
  And folks did at her gape.

She carried in her hand a glass
  That made all things look large;—
Held it before the eyes of all
  Without the slightest charge.

She clothed herself in flowing robes,
  As doth a fairy queen;
And on them were the heads of imps
  And spectors, red and green.

She wore a wild distracted look—
  Miss Fancy was her name--
She led each mortal to this place
  Without one bit of shame.

And when she'd led them to this place
  And they'd thrown down their lot,
She'd disappear to make believe
  She'd not been in the plot.

I saw a lot of people there
  And all of them I knew;
Some came from out the cities near,
  Some from the distant "Soo."

They'd rather not had me about,
  But still I lingered near
And saw what each one threw away;
  The sight was droll yet drear.

One man threw down his poverty,
  Then ran as if for life;
Another dropped a tight closed sack,
  And in it was—his wife.

And then a lot of lovers came
  With burdens of all kinds
Made up of passion, darts and hate.
  Some came with feeble minds.

But these laid not their troubles down,
  When once they saw the heap;
Instead, they took them back again;
  I guess they thought they'd keep.

And then I saw old women come
  And throw their wrinkles down,
Perhaps they thought it made them
    young;
  But wrinkles are a crown.

Young women came, stripped off their
   tan;
  Some threw their feet away;
Perhaps they were a little large,
   I did not hear them say.

I saw a heap of noses red;
  A pile of ugly lips;
A lot of nasty rusty teeth;
  Some old disjointed hips.

But what surprised me most of all
  Was that this monstrous heap
Was built of things that were not sins,
  And things we all might keep.

But oh, what fools we mortals are!
  We know 'tis good that wins;
And yet we'll wear our longest coat
  To cover up our sins.

I noticed one throw down the hump,
  That grew upon his back;
And one. a very wicked man,
  Threw down his mem'ry sack.

Some folks threw down their modesty;
  Fine folks threw down their spleen;
A few threw ignorance away;
  None, passion black or green.

Now when the whole race of mankind
  Had cast their burdens down,
Miss Phantom took me by surprise—
  She played me for a clown.

She held her magnifying glass
  So I could see my face;
I fairly wilted at the sight
  Of such outlandish grace.

One way it seemed to be too short,
  The other way too wide:
My nose seemed just a little long;
  My mustache, it looked dyed.

I threw my face off in disgust;
  But luckily for me
Another just then did the same;
  To trade we did agree.

I took his face and put it on,
  Great horrors! what a sight!
I dare say 'twas a foot too long,
  And uglier than night.

He had some trouble with my face,
  I don't know what it was;
But when I got it back again
  Somehow it seemed to buzz.

And now I saw, with pleasure great,
  All species of mankind
Delivered from their grievances;
  But some had fault to find.

They stood and looked around the heap
   And said they didn't see
But what the things some threw away,
   To them would pleasures be.

So, as they looked and found this fault,
   A voice was heard to say,
" You all are now at liberty
   To change without delay."

At this, Miss Fancy came around
   And worked with might and main
To give each one some other pack:
   She used her glass again.

Some observations now I made
   While looking round about,
I saw a slave that had worn chains,
   Instead take up the gout.

But by the changes of his face
   I know he felt chagrin.
He looked as if he'd lost a friend,—
   Perhaps his nearest kin.

It was amusing, quite, to see
   Exchanges that were made:
Oft illness went for poverty,
   And pain with ease would trade.

The female world, amongst themselves,
   Began exchange of looks.
But I can't tell you all they did,
   In less than seven books.

But though they changed for this and
　　that,
　They were not satisfied:
One got a boil for some gray hair,
　Then sat her down and cried.

This seemed to be about the fact
　In every person's case;
For all were splut'ring over faults:
　Their ills seemed out of place.

Perhaps 'tis different with those
　Who evils long have had;
They grow accustomed to their hurt
　And think them not so bad.

At last all had the heap picked up;
　They made a piteous sight
While wandering up and down the plain
　In such a sorry plight.

From every side came loud complaints
　And murmurs of all kinds,
Deep groans and lamentations drear—
　Express of wretched minds.

Again the voice was heard to speak,
　And this is what it said:—
"Go cast those burdens down again!
　I'll give you yours instead."

At this, Miss Fancy disappeared,
　But in her stead was sent
The goddess Patience, whom we love
　Because she spreads content.

This goddess wore neat fitting dress—
　Was earnest and serene;
And when she looked toward the sky,
　Her smiling face was seen.

When each had laid his burden down,
　She stood beside the heap;
It shrank up to one-third its size—
　Some turned away to weep.

She gave to each his proper load;
　And also knowledge how
To bear it most commodious,
　And too, to pay life's vow.

They all marched off contentedly,
　So grateful now to know
That they had not the thing they chose,—
　Some other person's woe.

All this has taught me to be wise,
　As well I think it might;
And not to envy or repine
　At morn, or noon, or night.

The smoke from chimneys all around
  Would scarcely swerve to left or right;
And birds would cluster in the trees
  As if to take their yearly flight.

As noon drew near, a whit'ning veil
  Would dim the form of distant hills
Then slowly spread, in subtle stealth,
  Enshrouding land, and lakes, and rills.

And now, at first, a stray flake fell,—
  An indistinct approaching speck
Slow-circling, edging t'ward the ground,
  As if it could the earth bedeck.

But soon you'd see another fall;
  Another, and another one,
With motion as it pleased them best,—
  As men come home when work is done.

Then faster come and larger grow
  The flakes. And now thick clouds of
    snow
For half an hour in hurry fall,
  And then the wind begins to blow.

The day declines; the snow grows dense;
  The wind increases hour by hour;
Until outside like one great tent
  Is spread the snow o'er Nature's bow'r

And trav'lers, meeting on the road,
  Each other hardly see or hear;
For sight and sound have little scope
  In such a snow-filled atmosphere.

The passing train, half mile away,
  Scarce makes its screeching whistle
    heard;
And if a forest tree should fall,
  You would not know it had occurred.

The sun goes down; the darkness comes;
  A wild confusion then ensues;
And drifting, whirling, darting snow,
  Awakes a spirit of " the blues."

Around the corners whips the wind
  A moaning, groaning as it goes;
And seeking crevice, nick and crack,
  Adds all it can to poor men's woes.

❧ ❧ ❧

To Cloa.

As I sit and watch kind sister
  By the bed of mother dear,
Years agone are softly speaking,
  Whisp'ring words into my ear.

And they tell me that when little,
  Mother sat and watched o'er me;
And that soon, among the roses,
  Her sweet face no more I'll see.

She has been the best of mothers,
  And I fain would bid her stay;
But the Angel Death must claim her
  Till the resurrection day.

Then upon that shore immortal,
  She the Saviour will adore;
And her face in angel beauty,
  We shall look upon once more.

But, dear sister, we will miss her
  During all our sojourn here;
And we shall be sad and lonely,
  Till the Life King shall appear.

Then there'll be a grand reunion:
  Friends that here have passed away
Will unite no more to sever
  In that grand eternal day.

Yes, my sister life is ebbing,
  But it will return some day;
So let's pray that when it cometh
  God will wipe our tears away.

It is sweet to have a mother
  Though she's old and feeble grown;
For her love outweighs the planets,
  All its depth cannot be known.

In this world, no bard or poet
　Can her praise too often sing;
For the living have their being
　By her love and nourishing.

This poem was written one night, several years ago
when mother was not expected to live. But I am happy
to state that she recovered and is still living.

Depression.

My soul, why art thou so oppressed?
Whence comes this boding, strange unrest?
What means this weight that bears thee
　　down?
What Fate is looking now with frown?

The time was glad but yesterday;
This morn, the heart was light and gay;
No wretched stomach casts the gloom;
No waning stimulant gives room

To such strange shadows, drear and cold,
As rise, like death-shapes, from the mold
Within the closure of a crypt
Where poison waters long have dripped.

'Tis like a frigid day and snow
That settles down when June buds blow;
Or like a bright midsummer day
By fierce midwinter chased away.

My friends are true,--what friends I care;
My love is true,—the letter, there,
Exhales perfume to sense and soul,
Nor breathes but trust in years to roll.

Yet in the years now far away
Where distant past is leaden gray,
Are tracings, made by crushing woes
That ruthless stalked, like giant foes,

O'er tender heart-buds' springtime bloom;
And many hopes lie in the tomb.
But not these graves themselves obtrude
And bind by melancholy mood.

These hallowed graves received warm tears;
And many flow'rs, in later years,
Have come above the sacred dead
To give a fragrant breath instead.

Ah, no! 'tis not the far or near
Of other days, nor insincere,
Inconstant ones of present day,
That drives the cheerful thoughts away.

The gloom is pressed by taunting gnomes
Whose wings now shade, who knows what
    homes?
And gladness glides from where they lurk,
Chased by their cry, " No work! no work!"

                                        *

A Reply.

After the day has sung its song of sorrow,
  No more remember it was sad and drear;
For it is so: the sun somewhere is shining
  And in our lives its radiance will appear.
How fair the day when love is overflowing!
  How bright the blossom rising in our
    hearts!
Dear love! 'tis love that makes the world all
  joyous;
  And life has nothing fairer it imparts.
See, love, I come! my feet are light with
  gladness;
  For love and life their beauty overcast.
And now I speak though all the lonely
  silence,
  "Hope on dear heart, our lives shall meet at
    last."

Oh it was long, the heavy day of sorrow.
  The hours seem long until we meet again.
But all the way is flooded now with sunshine
  And life is voicing Love's melodic strain.
From near, from far, the harpers all are
  merry—
  The music forms like countless flowers
    ablow:
And fairy shapes, with rose and perfume,
  gaily

Are passing on the breezes to and fro.
Thus earth is changed and heav'n is brought
    to mortals:
And so we wish life never will be past;
And filled with love, my heart speaks to you
    ever,
"Hope on dear heart, our lives shall meet at
    last."
                          *

❧ ❧ ❧

Won't You Be My Bride?

[Song.]

A winsome Miss of twenty,
  A lad just twenty-three,
With hammock went one evening
  To swing beneath a tree.
Of course to keep her near him,
  His arm around her strayed;
And softly he kept saying -
  Saying as they swayed:

CHORUS.
Won't you be my bride, dear?
  I love you!
Be what I am asking,
  O, please do.
Listen to my pleadings;
  Don't say nay.
Won't you be my bride, dear?
  Answer yea.

One year these two had courted;
  And so while by her side
He thought 'twere well to ask her
  If she would be his bride.
The hammock stopped its swinging;
  He knelt close at her feet;
And when he'd told his story,
  These words he did repeat:

CHORUS.

Two years have passed since swinging
  That lovely summer night.
He's sitting in the parlor
  Where all is gay and bright;
His wife is bending o'er him,
  A smile upon her face;
For he once more is singing,
  While holding baby Grace:

CHORUS.

Memory Gems.

Merry coming merry going,
  Days are long or days are short,
But with music, they forever
  Keep with Friendship s bright cohort.

*

Shall I forget so true a friend
   And all the many hours
That, like a summer day, has lived
   In Friendship's realm of flow'rs?
Though other hours will come and go
   And other friends be near
I'll prize the fair forget-me-not
   That brightly blossomed here.   *

———

Smile, when the sky is clear;
   Smile, when the sky is glum;
Smile, when the day is bright;
   Smile, when the night is come;
Smile, when you've many friends;
   Smile, though you know of none;
Smile, all the days of life;
   Thus is the triumph won.   *

———

"Those that toil bravely are strongest,"
   Was said long, long ago.
And it fights my hardest battles
   And gives me joy for woe.

www.ingramcontent.com/pod-product-compliance
Lightning Source LLC
Chambersburg PA
CBHW030912260626
47169CB00008B/2805